T0417635

SUPERHERO SCIENCE

INVISIBILITY

BY BLAKE HOENA

BELLWETHER MEDIA • MINNEAPOLIS, MN

Blastoff! Discovery launches a new mission: reading to learn. Filled with facts and features, each book offers you an exciting new world to explore!

BLASTOFF! UNIVERSE

BLASTOFF! Beginners — GRADE K

BLASTOFF! READERS — GRADES 1-3

BLASTOFF! DISCOVERY — GRADE 4

This edition first published in 2021 by Bellwether Media, Inc.

No part of this publication may be reproduced in whole or in part without written permission of the publisher.
For information regarding permission, write to Bellwether Media, Inc.,
Attention: Permissions Department,
6012 Blue Circle Drive, Minnetonka, MN 55343.

Library of Congress Cataloging-in-Publication Data

Names: Hoena, B. A., author.
Title: Invisibility / by Blake Hoena.
Description: Minneapolis, MN : Bellwether Media, Inc., 2021. | Series:
    Blastoff! discovery : superhero science | Includes bibliographical
    references and index. | Audience: Ages 7-13 | Audience: Grades 4-6 |
Summary: "Engaging images accompany information about the science of
    invisibility. The combination of high-interest subject matter and
    narrative text is intended for students in grades 3 through 8"–Provided
    by publisher.
Identifiers: LCCN 2020017993 (print) | LCCN 2020017994 (ebook) | ISBN
    9781644872604 (library binding) | ISBN 9781681037233 (ebook)
Subjects: LCSH: Invisibility–Juvenile literature. | Metamaterials–Juvenile literature.
    | Camouflage (Biology)–Juvenile literature. | Superheroes–Juvenile literature.
Classification: LCC QC406 .H64 2021 (print) | LCC QC406 (ebook) |
    DDC 535–dc23
LC record available at https://lccn.loc.gov/2020017993
LC ebook record available at https://lccn.loc.gov/2020017994

Editor: Elizabeth Neuenfeldt   Designer: Jeffrey Kollock

Printed in the United States of America, North Mankato, MN.

TABLE OF CONTENTS

THE INVISIBLE WOMAN

INVISIBLE
WOMAN

4

There is trouble in the streets of New York City. Doctor Doom is on the loose. He is one of the greatest villains that the Fantastic Four have faced. Now he is out to destroy the city!

Thankfully, the Fantastic Four are here to save the day! But the team needs to act fast. They decide someone needs to sneak up on Doctor Doom. Three of the heroes turn to their fourth team member, Sue Storm. In the blink of an eye, she disappears. She is the Invisible Woman!

MEET THE TEAM

▶ The Fantastic Four also includes the Human Torch, the Thing, and Mr. Fantastic. The Human Torch can fly and shoot fireballs. The Thing has super tough skin and super strength. Mr. Fantastic can stretch out his body!

The rest of the Fantastic Four jump into action. They begin to attack Doctor Doom and **distract** him. Meanwhile, the Invisible Woman is **translucent** as she sneaks toward the supervillain. Doctor Doom looks her way. But he sees nothing. He continues to battle the other three heroes.

Just as Doctor Doom prepares an attack, the Invisible Woman strikes. Unseen, she creates an **force field** around the supervillain. He is trapped inside an invisible barrier! The Invisible Woman saved the team and the city!

SUPERHERO FAMILY

▶ **Creator Stan Lee wanted the Fantastic Four to have a family-like bond. The Invisible Woman is the Human Torch's sister. She is also married to Mr. Fantastic. They are close friends with the Thing!**

7

UNSEEN SUPERHEROES

MARTIAN MANHUNTER

WONDER WOMAN

The power of invisibility makes superheroes unseen to others. Since the earliest comic books, there have been invisible superheroes. In 1939, the Invisible Hood first appeared in DC Comics. He wears a robe covered in a special chemical. While wearing the robe, the Invisible Hood vanishes!

In the 1940s, DC's Wonder Woman began using an invisible jet to travel undetected! Later, DC introduced Martian Manhunter. He is an alien from Mars. He was born with many **abilities**, including invisibility!

8

JUSTICE LEAGUE

▶ Martian Manhunter and Wonder Woman are two of the original members of DC Comics' Justice League. This team has fought villains to protect Earth since 1960!

MEDIA MANIA!

MOVIE

The Hobbit: An Unexpected Journey

YEAR 2012

DESCRIPTION

Based on J.R.R. Tolkien's book *The Hobbit*, the movie follows a hobbit named Bilbo Baggins who finds a mysterious ring deep down in a cavern. When he wears the ring, he becomes invisible! Bilbo uses this ring to sneak up on the dragon Smaug!

Marvel Comics made invisible heroes, too! The Invisible Woman made her first appearance in 1961. She disappears by turning herself translucent. In 1963, Marvel created Doctor Strange. He is a **sorcerer**. He uses magic to be invisible!

DOCTOR
STRANGE

IRON MAN
SUITS

RADAR

240
230
130

In the same year, Marvel introduced Iron Man. To be unseen, he created his own **stealth** Iron Man suit. It uses special technology that bends **radio waves** around the suit. This makes him invisible to **radar** devices that detect flying objects!

11

Some heroes have been introduced more recently. In 2004, Pixar made a movie about a superhero family called *The Incredibles*. Violet, the oldest child in the family, can make herself disappear! She can also create force fields like the Invisible Woman. But Violet's force fields are colored purple.

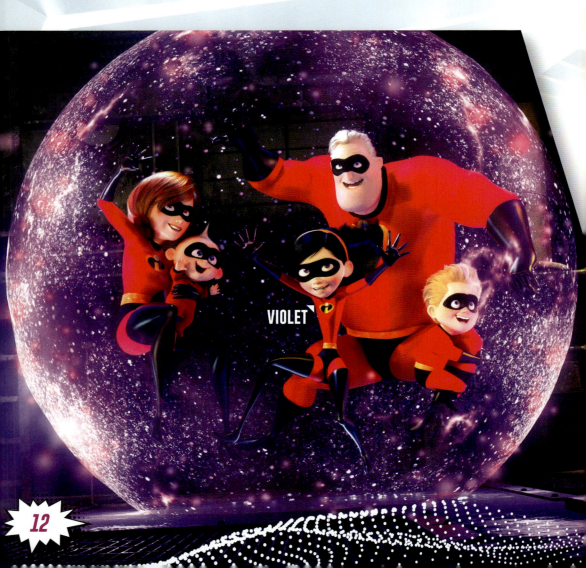

VIOLET

SUPERHERO PROFILE

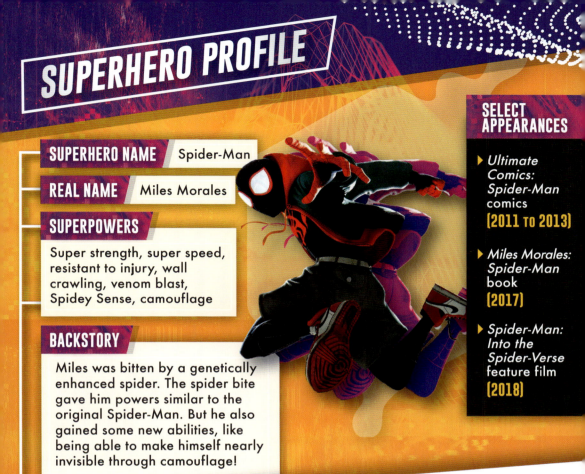

SUPERHERO NAME Spider-Man

REAL NAME Miles Morales

SUPERPOWERS

Super strength, super speed, resistant to injury, wall crawling, venom blast, Spidey Sense, camouflage

BACKSTORY

Miles was bitten by a genetically enhanced spider. The spider bite gave him powers similar to the original Spider-Man. But he also gained some new abilities, like being able to make himself nearly invisible through camouflage!

SELECT APPEARANCES

▸ *Ultimate Comics: Spider-Man* comics **[2011 TO 2013]**

▸ *Miles Morales: Spider-Man* book **[2017]**

▸ *Spider-Man: Into the Spider-Verse* feature film **[2018]**

In 2011, Marvel introduced a new version of Spider-Man. His name is Miles Morales. Like the original Spider-Man, he has a Spidey Sense and can swing from webs. But he also can **camouflage** himself. This makes it hard for others to see him!

EVERYDAY INVISIBILITY

STEALTH AIRCRAFT

RADAR

RADAR ANTENNA

Invisibility is not just a thing of comic books. There are ways people and objects can go unseen. One way is through stealth technology on aircraft. Stealth technology keeps aircraft from being detected by radar.

Radar devices track airplanes by sending out radio waves. These waves bounce off an airplane's body and back to the radar device. But stealth aircraft are built to absorb and reflect radar **signals** so they do not return to the radar device. This helps military aircraft go undetected in enemy territory.

SNEAKY AIRCRAFT

▶ The F-117 Nighthawk fighter-bomber jet was the first airplane to use stealth technology. The aircraft completed its first flight in 1981!

HOW STEALTH TECHNOLOGY WORKS

1 A radar device sends out radio waves to search for aircraft

2 Radio waves reach stealth aircraft

3 Angled edges on the plane reflect some radio waves so they cannot return to radar device

4 Special black paint that covers the plane absorbs some radio waves

Camouflage is another way people can become invisible. For example, soldiers dress in uniforms and use vehicles that match the colors of their surroundings. Green is used in forested areas. Tan is common in deserts. There are even white uniforms for snowy areas.

INVISIBILITY IN NATURE

ANIMALS HAVE WAYS OF HIDING THEMSELVES, WHETHER THEY ARE TRYING TO SNEAK UP ON PREY OR HIDE FROM A PREDATOR.

MOON JELLYFISH

TRANSLUCENT BODIES MAKE THEM HARD TO SEE IN WATER

CHAMELEONS

CHANGE THE COLOR OF THEIR SKIN TO LOOK LIKE THEIR SURROUNDINGS

SNOW CAMOUFLAGE

Military uniforms and vehicles are also covered in unique patterns. These patterns **mimic** the splotches of color found in nature. This helps soldiers and vehicles to blend into their surroundings and stay hidden.

MAKING INVISIBILITY A REALITY

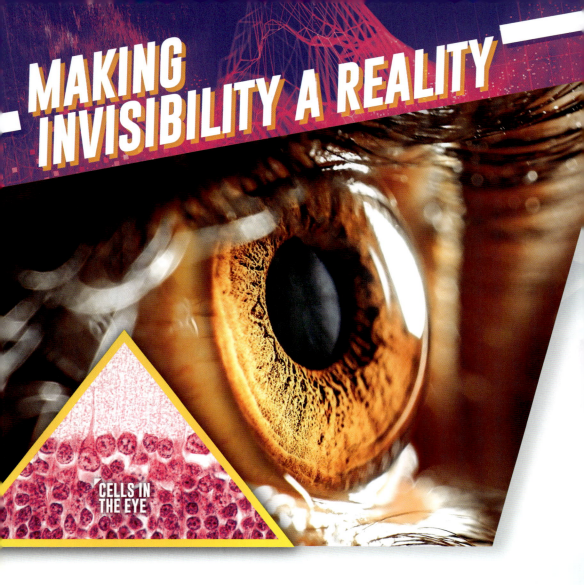

CELLS IN THE EYE

Invisibility seems like a great superpower to have.
An invisible person could move around unseen by others.
In reality, an invisible person would not see anything at all!

For people to see, there must be light. Light **particles** reflect off things and travel to a person's eye. The **cells** in the eye sense light particles and send signals to the brain. The brain **interprets** these signals so the person knows what they are seeing. If someone became invisible, light particles would not reach their eyes. The cells that sense light would not sense anything. Everything would look pitch black!

NEGATIVE EFFECTS OF INVISIBILITY ON HUMANS

CELLS IN EYES CANNOT SENSE LIGHT

EFFECT: ▸ BLINDNESS

INVISIBLE PERSON CAN BECOME INJURED OR ILL

EFFECT: ▸ A DOCTOR CAN NOT TREAT INJURIES OR ILLNESSES

INVISIBLE PERSON EMITS SMELL OR MAKES SOUND

EFFECT: ▸ COULD BE SPOTTED BY OTHER PEOPLE

REFRACTION

True invisibility may not be possible. This is because all naturally clear materials, such as glass, **refract** light. When light particles pass through a glass of water, they move slower than they do though air. When the light particles change speed, they bend. As a result, people can see through the glass of water. But the things behind it look **distorted**.

If someone became clear like water, they would still be visible. Other people would see a distortion in the shape of a human body.

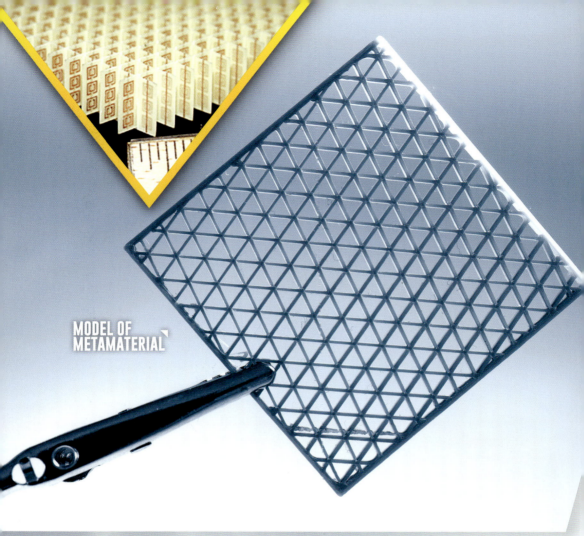

MODEL OF
METAMATERIAL

To combat refraction, scientists have created **artificial** materials called **metamaterials**. Metamaterials greatly reduce light refraction. They change the direction of light particles so the particles do not reach metamaterials. When light moves around metamaterials, whatever they cover becomes invisible!

MEASURING REFRACTION

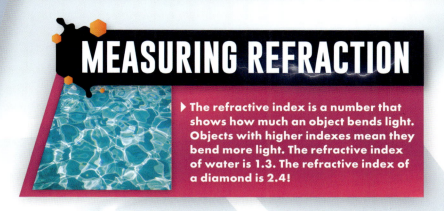

The refractive index is a number that shows how much an object bends light. Objects with higher indexes mean they bend more light. The refractive index of water is 1.3. The refractive index of a diamond is 2.4!

So far, scientists have only made small, flat things invisible with metamaterials. This is because it is hard to control how light particles move. But scientists continue to experiment with metamaterials to make larger things disappear.

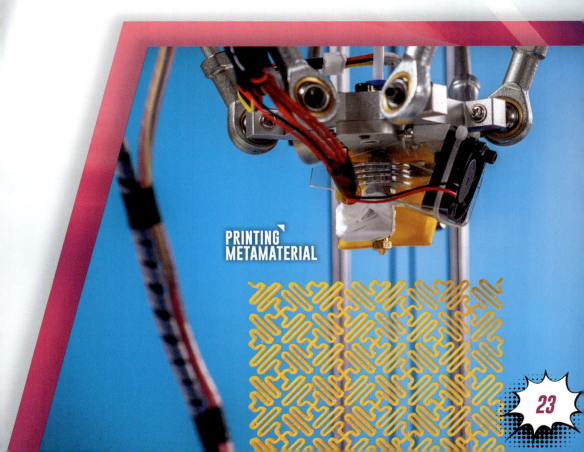

PRINTING METAMATERIAL

23

Scientists have also tried using cameras to turn people invisible. In 2003, Susumu Tachi made a cloak with **retroreflective** materials. A camera recorded everything behind the person wearing the cloak. Then, the video was **projected** onto the retroreflective cloak. The cloak acted like a movie screen to make the wearer disappear!

SUSUMU TACHI

RETROREFLECTIVE MATERIAL

24

RETROREFLECTIVE
CLOAK

But the cloak only worked if someone looked at it straight on. If someone saw the cloak from the side, they would simply see a person wearing a cloak! The bulky camera and projector could not move with the cloak.

THE FUTURE OF INVISIBILITY

Although people cannot turn themselves invisible, scientists are still finding ways to make things disappear. They are creating technology to hide the amount of **infrared light** a person **emits**. Infrared light cannot be seen by the human eye. But infrared cameras see this type of light. Militaries use these cameras to see people at night or when people wear camouflage. Infrared cameras even detect people inside a building!

In 2018, scientists created a sheet to reduce the amount of infrared light people emit. It could make it harder for soldiers to be seen on infrared cameras!

PERSON ON
INFRARED CAMERA

INFRARED BINOCULARS

27

ADAPTIV
SYSTEM

Militaries are also trying to hide vehicles from infrared cameras. Recently, scientists made a camouflage system called ADAPTIV. Vehicles are covered in hexagon-shaped materials that are heated or cooled to change how a vehicle emits infrared light. ADAPTIV could make a giant tank look like a cow on infrared cameras!

Invisibility may only be possible in comic books. But many technologies help people blend into the world in different ways. One day, humans may discover how to become truly invisible!

STEER   10to30°C   HFG

ADAPTIV ON
INFRARED CAMERA

GLOSSARY

abilities—powers to do things

artificial—referring to something that is not natural; artificial materials are often made by humans.

camouflage—to use color or patterns to blend in with surroundings

cells—the smallest units of living things

distorted—altered or changed in a visible way

distract—to draw a person's attention or thoughts to something else

emits—produces and sends out

force field—an invisible barrier that can block objects from passing through it

infrared light—a type of light that people cannot see; infrared light is often associated with heat emissions.

interprets—understands in a certain way

metamaterials—artificial materials that reduce refraction

mimic—to copy something or someone very closely

particles—the tiniest parts of things

projected—caused to appear on a surface; projectors make images appear on screens.

radar—a radio device that uses radio waves to determine the position and direction of moving objects

radio waves—invisible waves used to send signals through the air without using wires

refract—to bend, alter, or distort

retroreflective—related to a type of material that reflects light particles directly back; traffic signs and lines on roads are retroreflective.

signals—messages that serve to start some action

sorcerer—a person who practices magic

stealth—related to technology used to hide vehicles from radar

translucent—clear enough to allow light to pass through

TO LEARN MORE

AT THE LIBRARY

Hirschmann, Kris. *The Science of Super Powers: An Incredibles Discovery Book*. Minneapolis, Minn.: Lerner Publications, 2020.

MacCarald, Clara. *What Would It Take to Make an Invisibility Cloak?* North Mankato, Minn.: Capstone Press, 2020.

Scirri, Kaitlin. *The Science of Invisibility and X-ray Vision*. New York, N.Y.: Cavendish Square, 2019.

ON THE WEB

FACTSURFER

Factsurfer.com gives you a safe, fun way to find more information.

1. Go to www.factsurfer.com.

2. Enter "invisibility" into the search box and click 🔍.

3. Select your book cover to see a list of related content.

INDEX